For our moms and our dads, who always
made sure we were nourished and well fed

Copyright © 2015 by Dean Hacohen and Sherry Scharschmidt

First edition 2015

Library of Congress Catalog Card Number 2013957481
ISBN 978-0-7636-6586-9

15 16 17 18 19 20 LEO 10 9 8 7 6 5 4 3 2 1
Printed in Heshan, Guangdong, China

This book was typeset in Journal and Providence Sans.
The illustrations were created digitally.

Candlewick Press
99 Dover Street
Somerville, Massachusetts 02144

visit us at www.candlewick.com

Who's Hungry?

Dean Hacohen &
Sherry Scharschmidt

CANDLEWICK PRESS

Time to eat.
Is anybody hungry?

Glad you like it, Bunny.
Who else is hungry?

I am! I would love
a fresh fish, please.

You're quick, Seal!
Who else is hungry?

I am! Bananas are
my favorite.

I am!
I like to eat hay.

I am! I would like
an acorn, please.

I am! I can't wait to chew some bamboo.

I am! May I have
some cheese, please?

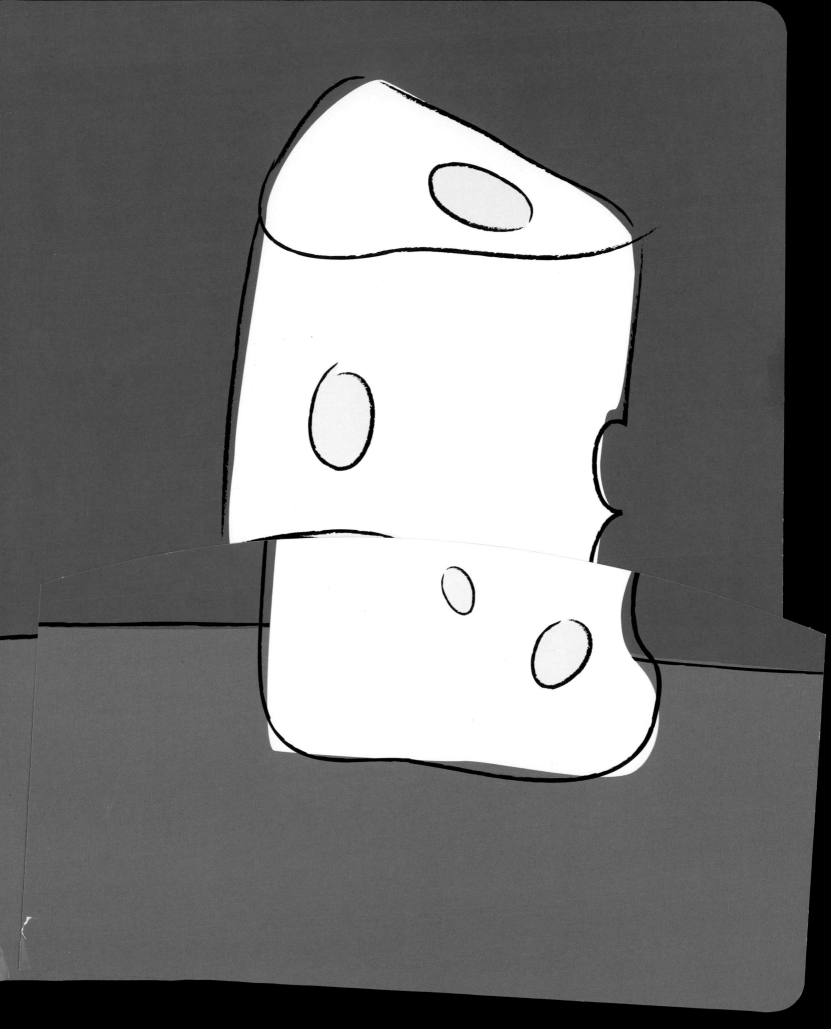

Are you?
Eat up!